Wake Up, Crabby!

🌰 ACORN™

SCHOLASTIC INC.

For Floralei, my early morning drawing buddy.

Library of Congress Cataloging-in-Publication Data

Names: Fenske, Jonathan, author, illustrator.
Title: Wake up, Crabby! / Jonathan Fenske.
Description: First edition. | New York, NY : Acorn/Scholastic Inc., 2019. | Series: A Crabby book ; 3 | Summary: It is late and Crabby just wants to sleep, but Plankton keeps Crabby awake with questions and chatter—until a request for a bedtime story takes an unexpected turn.
Identifiers: LCCN 2018060386 | ISBN 9781338281613 (pbk. : alk. paper) | ISBN 9781338281637 (hardcover : alk. paper)
Subjects: LCSH: Crabs—Juvenile fiction. | Plankton—Juvenile fiction. | Bedtime—Juvenile fiction. | Storytelling—Juvenile fiction. | CYAC: Crabs—Fiction. | Plankton—Fiction. | Bedtime—Fiction. | Humorous stories.
Classification: LCC PZ7.F34843 Wak 2019 | DDC (E)—dc23 LC record available at https://lccn.loc.gov/2018060386

10 9 8 7 6 5 4 3 2   19 20 21 22 23

Printed in China   62

First edition, November 2019
Edited by Katie Carella
Book design by Maria Mercado

THE DREAM

Tonight is just another night at the beach.

It is enough to make a crab **crabby**.

And **sleepy**.

3

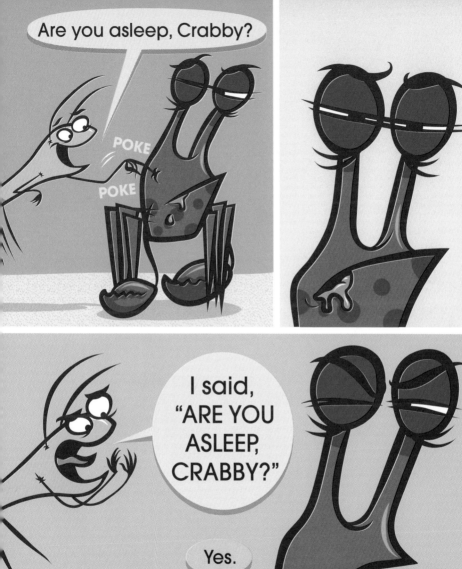

5

Oh. Okay.

Wait a second.

Are you **sure** you are asleep?

Yes. I am sure.

6

8

9

OKAY, OKAY! I AM NOT ASLEEP!

Well, you **should** be asleep. It is very late.

THE BATH

Hey, Crabby! I just took the **best** bedtime bath!

Yippee.

11

Do you want to smell like a **stinky crab**?

News flash: I **am** a stinky crab.

What if it was a nice hot bubble bath?

Sea creatures should not **take** nice hot bubble baths.

Why not?

Ask Lobster.

Poppa?

But look at all the shiny bubbles!

TAP
TAP

TWITCH
TWITCH

WILL YOU PLEASE JUST TAKE A BATH?

Fine, Plankton. You **really** want me to take a bath?

Yes!

Then I will **take** a bath.

Yay!

17

But you cannot **watch** me take a bath!

Silly me!

SMACK!

19

All done!

Wow! That was fast!

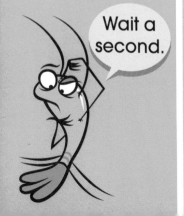

Wait a second.

Where is the bath?

21

THE SONG

25

Sigh.

I guess I will not hear a bedtime song.

Wow. It sure is quiet.

Sure is.

Some might say it is **too** quiet.

Okay, Plankton. I get it. You want me to sing you a bedtime song.

I sure do!

29

32

So, if I tell you a bedtime story, you will go to sleep?

Yes!

Do you **promise**?

I promise.

Then I will tell you a bedtime story.

Yay!

There were two best friends.

Me and you?

Their names were Whale and Plankton.

Oh.

They did **everything** together.

Like me and you!

35

They **sunned** in the sun.

Aaah.

They had a wonderful time together.

Woo-hoo!

Then Whale got hungry.

Poor Whale!

Whale's tummy **rumbled**.

RUMBLE RUMBLE

Time to eat!

Whale's tummy **grumbled**.

GRUMBLE GRUMBLE

Get that Whale some food!

38

41

Do they?

They might if they were really, really hungry.

Gulp.

Crabby, are **you** really, really hungry?

No, silly! I am not really, really hungry.

Phew.

About the Author

Jonathan Fenske lives in South Carolina with his family. He was born in Florida near the ocean, so he knows all about life at the beach! He likes to wake up early, and he **loves** bubble baths and bedtime stories.

Jonathan is the author and illustrator of several children's books including **Barnacle Is Bored**, **Plankton Is Pushy** (a Junior Library Guild selection), and the LEGO® picture book **I'm Fun, Too!** His early reader **a Pig, a Fox, and a Box** was a Theodor Seuss Geisel Honor Book.

YOU CAN DRAW DUCKIE!

QUACK!

1. Draw a leaning figure eight.

2. Connect the circles with a line to make the body and tail.

3. Add a beak and a feather on top.

4. Erase the leftover parts of the circles.

5. Draw a circle and dot for the eye and a scribble for the wing.

6. Color in your drawing!

WHAT'S YOUR STORY?

Plankton loves to take baths with Duckie.

Do **you** like to take baths?

Would your bath have lots of bubbles or no bubbles?

What is your favorite bath toy?

Write and draw your story!